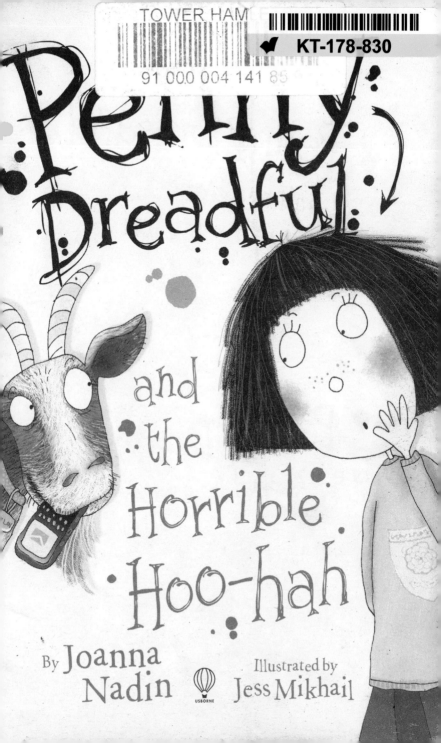

KT-178-830

Penny Dreadful

and the Horrible Hoo-hah

By Joanna Nadin

USBORNE

Illustrated by Jess Mikhail

Contents

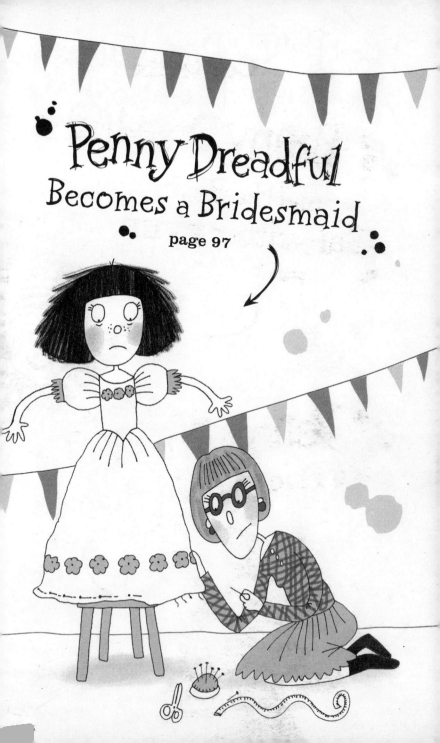

Penny Dreadful
Becomes a Bridesmaid

page 97

Meet Penny Dreadful and her Resigned Relations...

Penny
(It's never really her fault...)

Georgia May Morton-Jones
(Penny's clever cousin)

Cosmo
(Penny's best friend)

Daisy
(Penny's annoying sister)

Penny's long-suffering **mum** and **dad**

Very prim-and-proper **Aunt Deedee**

Barry
(Miaow, I'm Gran's cat)

Gran
(Normally found fast asleep somewhere)

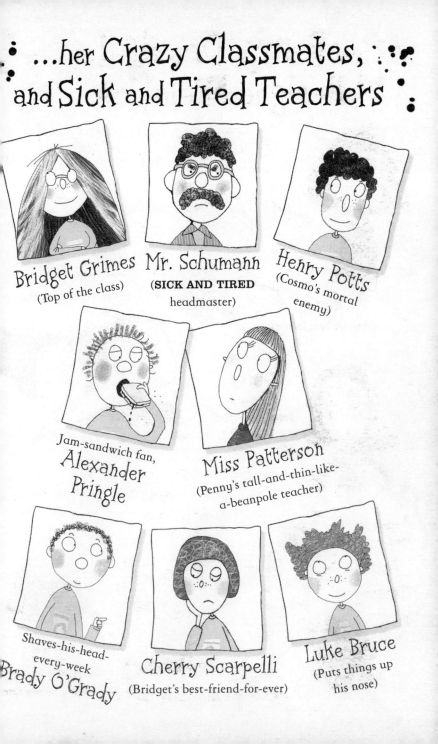

...her Crazy Classmates, and Sick and Tired Teachers

Bridget Grimes
(Top of the class)

Mr. Schumann
(**SICK AND TIRED** headmaster)

Henry Potts
(Cosmo's mortal enemy)

Jam-sandwich fan,
Alexander Pringle

Miss Patterson
(Penny's tall-and-thin-like-a-beanpole teacher)

Shaves-his-head-every-week
Brady O'Grady

Cherry Scarpelli
(Bridget's best-friend-for-ever)

Luke Bruce
(Puts things up his nose)

Penny Dreadful
and the Best Babysitter Ever

My name is not actually
Penny Dreadful. It is Penelope Jones.
The "Dreadful" bit is my dad's
JOKE. I know it is a joke because
every time he says it he laughs
like a honking goose.

But I do not see the funny side. Plus it is not even true that I am dreadful. It is like Gran says, i.e. that I am a **MAGNET FOR DISASTER**. Mum says if Gran kept a better eye on me in the first place instead of on *Jack Be Nimble* in the two o'clock at Newmarket then I might not be quite so magnetic. But Gran says if Mum wasn't so busy answering phones for Dr. Cement, who is her boss, and who has bulgy eyes like hard-boiled eggs (which is why everyone calls him Dr. Bugeye), and Dad wasn't so busy solving crises at the council, then they would be able to solve some crises at 73 Rollins Road, i.e. our house. So you see it is completely not my fault.

✯ ✩ ✯ ✯

Sometimes it is the fault of my sister Daisy, who is very **IRRITATING**. And who is especially irritating when she is trying to be a pop star with her best friend Lucy B. Finnegan, because they are mostly arguing over who is going to be the main singer and who is going to do swaying hips and doo-wops, e.g. going "I am", "No I am", "No I am". So it is not my fault if I borrow the microphone while they are arguing to see if it works under water and it does not.

And sometimes it is the fault of Cosmo Moon Webster, who is my best friend even though he is a week older than me and a boy. Because if it wasn't for his mum Sunflower (who is actually called Barbara) being so **KEEN** on **FREEDOM** and **SELF-EXPRESSION**, then we would not have been **FREE** to paint ourselves purple and pretend to be minions of Maximus Terror, leader of the Zombiebots. And then Mrs. Butterworth (who works in the post office and has a moustache and a beady eye, which is mostly on me) would not have had the **HEEBIE-JEEBIES** and had to go to see Dr. Cement for some tonic to recover.

And sometimes it is the fault of Dad, because he is mostly saying, e.g. *"I could have been an escapologist if I hadn't met your mum"*, only Mum says he could not because he cannot even find his way out of the one-way system, let alone a locked cage. And it turns out she is right because when I lock him in the bathroom he completely cannot undo the door and has to come out of the window in only a towel, which gives Mrs. Butterworth the **HEEBIE-JEEBIES** again and so it is back to Dr. Cement.

But this week it is the fault of someone else completely and that is Hilary O. Henderson, and also maybe Mum, who should have said:

a) No dressing as **HOOLIGANS**.

2. No dipping things in **HONEY** and **HUNDREDS AND THOUSANDS**.

iii) No using **MYSTERIOUS MONKEY HANDS**.

What happens is that normally I am not **KEEN** on babysitters because they are mostly old people with beady eyes and moustaches, like e.g. Mrs. Butterworth, who say no you **CANNOT** eat fourteen biscuits and then jump up and down on the sofa to see how long it is before you are sick, you can **SIT STILL** and read a book about otters.

And Mum is not keen on babysitters either because they are mostly old people with beady eyes and moustaches, like e.g. Mrs. Butterworth, who say, "In my day children knew the **MEANING** of the word **DISCIPLINE**." And Mum says **I DO** know the meaning, but she tests me and I do not, unless **DISCIPLINE** is a sort of a dinosaur. Which is

15

why it is either Gran who is left in charge, or if it is bingo night then no one goes out, because it is **NOT WORTH THE HOO-HAH**.

But on Saturday something **UNPREDICTABLE** happens which means no one knew it was coming (which I know because Miss Patterson, who is our teacher and who is tall and thin like a beanpole, said it was completely **UNPREDICTABLE** when the rubber I was throwing at Henry Potts, who is Cosmo's mortal enemy, pinged off a poster about potatoes and hit our headmaster Mr. Schumann on the ear just as he was coming into our class to tell us we had won Class of the Week for being excellent – only he changed his mind and it went to 3C who made a collage about cows, and I got a gold star taken away, which I said was unfair but Mum said was completely **PREDICTABLE**).

But this **UNPREDICTABLE** thing is even more **DISASTROUS** because it is that Mum and Dad have got to go to the Roundabout Ball and they cannot say no because Mr. Hobnob, who is Dad's boss and who has hair like a hedgehog, will **FROWN** on them, and he is already **FROWNING** on Dad for several things, i.e.:

1. Moving some traffic cones from one side of the road (which was the left side of the road) to the right side of the road (which was the **WRONG** side of the road).

b) Building a tower with a hole punch, a stapler and a machine-that-goes-beep, which collapsed and the machine-that-goes-beep knocked over a cup of tea that went spill, and it was all over an important picture of a parking meter.

3. Going to a crucial meeting about Belisha beacons in a helmet made of a flowerpot and a remote-control car, which was not completely my fault, it was a **PATENT BRAIN-MASSAGING HELMET**, only it was too small for Dad's enormous brain and got stuck.

And Gran has to go dancing with her friend Arthur Peason and she cannot say no because Arthur will **FROWN** on her, and he is already **FROWNING** on her for several things, i.e.:

a) Beating him at Texas Hold 'Em seventeen times, which she says was down to beginner's luck but Arthur says was down to the ace of spades in her right pocket.

ii) Eating his last chocolate digestive even though it was not Gran, it was her cat Barry, and even though Mum says it is **CAT BISCUITS AND CAT BISCUITS ONLY**.

3. Digging up George and Mildred, who are a dead rabbit and a dead guinea pig, which was not completely my fault, it was because I was being an archaeologist and I thought they were a baby two-headed dinosaur.

And Mrs. Butterworth says no she cannot babysit because she is still getting the sticky stuff out from last time. And nor can Mrs. Nugent and nor can Aunt Deedee, who says she would rather **PERISH**.

Daisy says she would rather **PERISH** than have a babysitter anyway, and we do not need one because she is eleven and big enough to babysit **ALL BY HERSELF** and she will be in charge of me and I will be on my **BEST BEHAVIOUR**, you will see.

Only I do not want to see because I am not **KEEN** on Daisy being **IN CHARGE** because she has already bossed me three times today, e.g.:

a) No you cannot be a pop star because you are too **SMALL** and your hair is **WEIRD**.

2. No you cannot have a pear drop because you are too **SMALL** and you have socks on your ears, which is **WEIRD**.

3. No you cannot borrow my old doll that does wee-wees because you are too **SMALL** and last time you made her drink red ink, which is **WEIRD**.

So I say I would rather **PERISH** than have Daisy as a babysitter. And luckily so would Mum, because she says she will ring her friend Janice Ham to see who she uses and cross her fingers that she is free **TONIGHT**.

23

Only Janice Ham uses Shaniqua Reynolds from the hairdresser's, who is at a plaiting convention in Chipping Sodbury, so she says to ring Felicity Minky.

Only Felicity Minky says she uses Kimberley Puttock, who has got a sore finger, so she says to ring Alexis Boreham-Best.

Only Alexis Boreham-Best says she uses Cosmo's mum Sunflower, who is doing a dance about the moon, so she says she will ask Cosmo's cousin Hilary, who is training to be a nanny, so it will be better than **BRILLIANT**. And Mum is not so sure because she does not think anything that involves Sunflower is **BETTER THAN BRILLIANT**, but as Gran says, **BEGGARS CAN'T BE CHOOSERS**, so it is Hilary who will be here at seven o'clock sharp.

★ ★ ★ ★

And so at 6.59 we are on **TENTERHOOKS** to see what Hilary will be like.

I say she is probably wearing a rainbow dress and will make us praise the sun and write poems about pixies.

Daisy says she is probably pierced on her nose and has purple hair and will not say a word except "Shut up and go to bed".

And Mum says she is probably **MAD** if she has agreed to come and babysit us two, but as long as she does not eat all the custard creams or blow the house to **SMITHEREENS**, then she does not care if she has purple hair or a pierced nose or makes us writes poems about pixies or elves or even Maximum Terror.

And before I can say it is Maxi*mus* Terror the doorbell goes. And I say,

Hurrah, it is Hilary.

Which it is. Only Hilary does not have purple hair or a pierced nose or a rainbow dress, or even a dress at all. Hilary has orangeish hair, and a T-shirt that says *Save the Whales*, and a beard – because Hilary is a **BOY**. Which is completely **UNPREDICTABLE** and Mum says so.

Hilary Who Is A Boy says,

It's a common mistake, but do not worry, I am almost completely qualified, and now it is time to shoo.

And I can tell Mum is about to say something about the shooing, or possibly about the T-shirt, but Dad says if they do not leave this **INSTANT**, Mr. Hobnob will do definite **FROWNING**, and Gran says if she doesn't leave this **INSTANT**, Arthur Peason will do definite **FROWNING**, so in comes Hilary Who Is A Boy and out shoos Mum and Dad and Gran.

And I am **INTERESTED** in Hilary Who Is
A Boy because I have never had a boy babysitter
before. And Daisy is also **INTERESTED** in Hilary
Who Is A Boy because she has scooted upstairs
and come back down in a completely different
dress and Rambling Rose lipstick, which she is
not supposed to wear except at a school disco
and I tell her so.

But she says,

Shut up.

And I say,

No, **YOU** shut up.

And she says,

No, **YOU** shut up!

And there is a lot of shut-upping

until Hilary Who Is A Boy says,

Instead of **SHUT-UPPING** let's play rock-paper-scissors and whoever wins will be **SUPREME CHAMPION** and then it will be decided.

SAVE THE

Which is when me and Daisy **SHUT UP** almost immediately, because we are both very **KEEN** on rock-paper-scissors and also on being **SUPREME CHAMPIONS**.

But Hilary Who Is A Boy says before we are **READY TO COMMENCE** we must go to the kitchen, because playing rock-paper-scissors requires concentration and concentration requires **SNACKS**, which we are also **KEEN** on. And so we go completely quickly to the kitchen and we get **SNACKS**, which are:

a) Some carrots

2. A jar of hundred and thousands

3. A jar of honey

Because Hilary Who Is A Boy says the only way to eat carrots is dipped in honey and hundreds and thousands, and for once me and Daisy agree. And so I say we are **READY TO COMMENCE**. But Hilary Who Is A Boy says in fact first we have to dress up as Hooligans because it is essential to dress as Hooligans when you are playing rock-paper-scissors and also eating carrots dipped in honey and hundreds and thousands. And the good thing about Hooligans is that they wear whatever they like as long as it is using their **IMAGINATIONS**, and then we will definitely be **READY TO COMMENCE**. And so me and Daisy and Hilary Who Is A Boy go upstairs and use our **IMAGINATIONS**.

And I **IMAGINE** a Hooligan who wears a shower curtain as a cape and a rubbish bin on my head (with the rubbish still in).

And Hilary Who Is a Boy **IMAGINES** a Hooligan who wears a pair of Gran's tights over his head and a swimming costume.

And Daisy **IMAGINES** a Hooligan who wears a pair of very tall heels and Mum's fake diamond necklace (which I know is fake because real diamonds do not crack if you bite them and I tested one once and it cracked and rolled under a radiator).

And then Hilary Who Is A Boy says we are all excellent Hooligans and so we are **READY TO COMMENCE** and so we do.

And to **COMMENCE** the **COMMENCING** we eat our snacks, and Hilary is right because honey and hundreds and thousands is the best way to eat carrots ever and even I do not complain and in fact then I have a **BRILLIANT IDEA™**, which is to test out other things to see if they are nice dipped in honey and hundreds and thousands, e.g.:

1. A bourbon, which is nice.

b) A pink wafer, which is nice.

3. A mini cheese, which is not nice, and even Barry agrees and he will eat pilchards.

And then next it is time to play rock-paper-scissors to decide who is **SUPREME CHAMPION**. And at first I am winning because I do scissors, and Daisy does paper, and so I cut her and I win.

And then Hilary Who Is A Boy does scissors, and I do rock, and so I blunt him and I win.

But then something else **UNPREDICTABLE** happens, which is that next time Daisy does paper, but Hilary Who Is A Boy does **MAGIC FINGER**, which is wiggling it in a circle, and so he has won. Only Daisy says **MAGIC FINGER** is not real so in fact she should have won, it is the rules (because Daisy is very keen on rules).

But Hilary
Who Is A Boy
says **MAGIC**
FINGER *is* real
and so is **FOOT**
OF DOOM,
which is
stamping very
hard on the
floor, and so is
MYSTERIOUS
MONKEY
HANDS, which
is waving them
around your
head like **MAD**.

And Daisy thinks in fact she is quite **KEEN** on **MAGIC FINGER** and **FOOT OF DOOM** and **MYSTERIOUS MONKEY HANDS** and so am I, and so we decide they are real and we can use them from now on, it is the rules.

And then Daisy wins the next go because she does **FOOT OF DOOM** and Hilary Who Is A Boy does **MAGIC FINGER** and so he is stamped on.

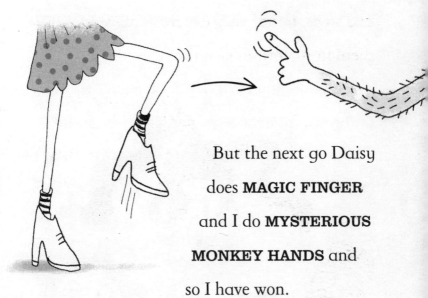

But the next go Daisy does **MAGIC FINGER** and I do **MYSTERIOUS MONKEY HANDS** and so I have won.

Only Daisy is not happy about this and pokes me with her **MAGIC FINGER**.

And so I use my **MYSTERIOUS MONKEY HANDS** to throw a mini cheese dipped in honey and hundreds and thousands at her **MAGIC FINGER**. Only it misses and hits Hilary Who Is A Boy on the nose

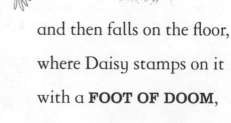

and then falls on the floor, where Daisy stamps on it with a **FOOT OF DOOM**, which is wearing a very high heel and so it is quite **DOOMY**.

And I say, "Forsooth, you have **SMITED** my mini cheese with your **FOOT OF DOOM** and so I will **SMITE** your necklace with my **MYSTERIOUS MONKEY HANDS**," which I do, because I am very **KEEN** on **SMITING** things. Only it turns out that everyone else is also very **KEEN** on **SMITING** things, e.g.:

i) Daisy says she will **SMITE** Hilary Who Is A Boy's Hooligan helmet of tights with a jar of honey, which she does.

2. Hilary Who Is A Boy says he will smite my Hooligan cloak with scissors, which are actual and not pretend ones from the game.

C) I say I will **SMITE** everything in the room with a jar of hundreds and thousands, which I do. Which is when something else **UNPREDICTABLE** happens, which is that Mum and Dad walk in.

And Daisy says,

Oops.

And Hilary
Who Is A
Boy says,

Crikey.

And I say,

It wasn't me.

But Mum says it was, because wherever there is a **HORRIBLE HOO-HAH**, there is me in the middle of it.

But I say,

It is not **HOO-HAH**, it is **HOOLIGANS** and also **FEET OF DOOM** and **MYSTERIOUS MONKEY HANDS**.

But Mum says she will be the judge of what is **HOO-HAH** and what is not and she judges it **IS**, and frankly it is the last thing she needs after a night trying to do the American Smooth with Mr. Hobnob, who is neither.

I say, but on the plus side we have not eaten all the custard creams and the house is not blown to **SMITHEREENS**, so in fact it is all alright.

But Mum does not agree and sends
Hilary O. Henderson home and sends me
and Daisy to bed without a snack, not even
a carrot dipped in honey.

Daisy says, "It is all your own fault, Penelope Jones, you are such a complete **MORON**." But I say it is not my fault, it is the fault of Hilary Who Is A Boy.

And for once Mum agrees, because the next time something **UNPREDICTABLE** happens, i.e. the Chipping Broadley Operatic Extravaganza, she decides she and Dad will stay in after all.

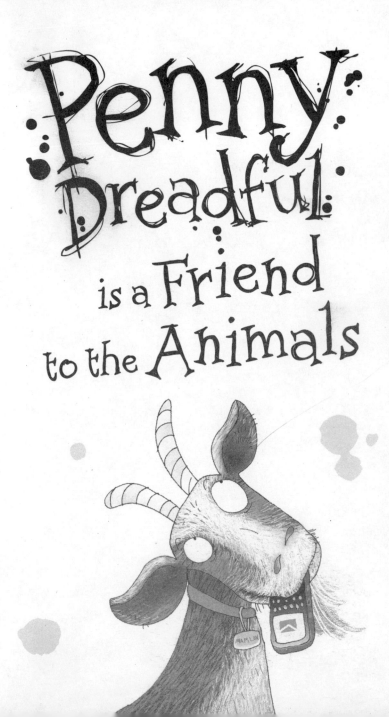

Penny Dreadful
is a Friend
to the Animals

Cosmo Moon Webster is my best friend

even though he is a
week older than me
and a boy because my
mum says we are like
TWO PEAS IN A POD,
i.e. completely and
exactly the same
because we both like
completely and exactly
the same things, i.e.:

a) Pink wafer biscuits.

2. Throwing e.g. rubbers at Henry Potts, who is Cosmo's mortal enemy.

iii) Inventing a time machine out of a bus, some tinfoil and an alarm clock.

d) *Animal SOS*, which is a programme on telly where animals nearly die and then they don't and it is **MIRACULOUS**.

5. Digging for buried treasure, e.g. a Roman coin and a mysterious key, which Mum says is not mysterious, it is the spare key to the back door which Dad buried in case we got locked out, only when we **DID** get locked out (which was not really my fault, I just wanted to see if the key fitted through the crack in the pavement), he forgot where he had buried the spare one so we had to break in with a golf club and a hammer.

But in fact we are not completely **PEA**-like because there is one big difference and that is that Cosmo is a vegetarian, i.e. he does not eat animals, not even one tiny bit of a chicken. This is because his mum Sunflower does not believe in eating anything that has been alive once, unless it is a carrot or a bit of broccoli or a squishy thing made of lentils, for instance. But I am **NOT** a vegetarian, because Mum says she is **UP TO HERE** with **FUSSY EATING**, because Daisy, who is my sister and who is very irritating, is being doubly irritating because she says she cannot eat cabbage as it is **AGAINST HER RELIGION**, and so is swede and soup and fish (unless it is fish fingers and chips). Dad says it is a very odd religion and Gran says it is a made-up religion and I say maybe I would like this religion because I am not **KEEN** on swede or soup either, but Mum says,

Oh for heaven's sake, it is **EAT WHAT YOU'RE GIVEN** and that is the end of it.

✫ ✫ ✫ ✫

Except it is not because the next day in assembly,

Mr. Schumann, who is our headmaster, and who

is normally saying things like "Penelope Jones,

I am **SICK** and **TIRED** of telling you that

sweetcorn is for swallowing, not pinging

at people", says something else,

and it is that from now on

there'll be Meat-Free

Mondays, which

means e.g.

vegetable goulash

for lunch instead

of sausages.

And almost immediately Cosmo jumps up and says

> Hurrah! It is a **VICTORY** for the animals!

But Mr. Schumann says it is not, it is a **VICTORY** for the council who are in charge of school dinners, and not to get too carried away and also to please sit down because Cosmo's silver wellies are distracting and it is time for Bridget Grimes (who is top of the class and Mr. Schumann's favourite) to play "All Things Bright and Beautiful" on the recorder.

Only when we get back to the classroom everyone is completely carried away with Meat-Free Monday, even Miss Patterson, because she says it is important to be interested in where food comes from, i.e. not the supermarket or the corner shop but fields and trees and farms, and it is especially important to be a **FRIEND TO THE ANIMALS**.

And Cosmo says he is **ALWAYS** a **FRIEND TO THE ANIMALS** because of being a vegetarian and also because he once

helped a worm out of a puddle with a ruler.

And then everyone is arguing like **MAD** about who is the best **FRIEND TO THE ANIMALS**, i.e.:

1. Alexander Pringle (who wears age 14 clothes even though he is nine because he is mostly eating jam sandwiches when he should not be eating jam sandwiches) says he once rescued a fly that was about to be eaten by a spider, so **HE** is the best **FRIEND TO THE ANIMALS**.

b) Bridget Grimes

says she once rescued a
spider that was about
to be eaten by a cat, so
SHE is the best **FRIEND**
TO THE ANIMALS.

3. Cherry Scarpelli (who is
Bridget Grimes's best friend, and who I have
seen eat a crayon) says she has rescued a cat

from the animal home
and it is called
Tallulah, so
SHE is the best
FRIEND TO
THE ANIMALS.

iv) Henry Potts says he has rescued a **DOG** from the animal home and it is called Optimus Prime, so **HE** is the best **FRIEND TO THE ANIMALS**.

e) Cosmo says he has rescued a **MONKEY** from the animal home and it is called Henry Potts, so **HE** is the best **FRIEND TO THE ANIMALS**.

Which is when Miss Patterson says it is nice that we are all so **INSPIRED**, but that is quite enough being **FRIENDS TO THE ANIMALS** for one day and it is time to open up our maths books instead and work out how many miles a car goes if it drives for ten minutes and is going thirty miles an hour and no it does not go round a roundabout seventeen times.

✦ ☆ ✦ ✦

But on the way home I have a

BRILLIANT IDEA™,

which is that I am going to be the best **FRIEND**

TO THE ANIMALS EVER and that maybe I can

go to the animal
home tomorrow and
rescue e.g. a rabbit or
a chicken or even an
otter. Only when I get
home Mum says **UNDER**
NO CIRCUMSTANCES
am I getting another
animal, not even
a **FISH**, because if

I get a pet then Daisy will want a pet, i.e. a pony because Lucy B. Finnegan has one, and Mum is already **UP TO HERE** with Barry, who is Gran's cat and who has just eaten four cream crackers and something with sticky stuff on it even though Mum says it is **CAT BISCUITS AND CAT BISCUITS ONLY**. Only I say,

But it is especially **IMPORTANT** because I want to be a **FRIEND TO THE ANIMALS**.

So Mum says if I am so **KEEN** on being a **FRIEND TO THE ANIMALS** I can start with Barry, because the sticky stuff has stuck him to the purple cushion and he is not at all **PLEASED** and nor is she because the noise is **INFERNAL**.

And so I unstick Barry, who is **PLEASED** again because he is not dragging a cushion around the floor, which is **GOOD DEED** number 1.

And all weekend I am doing more **GOOD DEEDS** to animals, i.e.:

1. I take Shaniqua Reynolds's dog Lennox for a walk to the shop and I only lose him two times.

b) I only eat two sausages at tea instead of three.

c) I give the spare sausage to Barry, who is **PLEASED AS PUNCH**.

4. I do not stamp on a wasp that is sitting on the patio looking like it might want to sting me at **ANY MINUTE** (only it does not, it wanders off towards Mrs. Nugent over the road, who hits it with a newspaper).

e) I collect fourteen beetles that are in the sandpit looking sad and give them a new home in a shoebox with some grass and some polystyrene peanuts and a sofa made of a matchbox.

And Dad says my beetle house
is a palace **FIT FOR A KING** and in
fact he could have been a zookeeper
if he hadn't met Mum, because he has
a **WAY** with animals. Only Mum says he does
not because he is scared of even a small snake,
plus the last time we went to the wildlife park
a monkey hit him on the hand. Only Dad
says that was not **HIS** fault, it was because
he was trying to rescue his sock. And I say
well that was not **MY** fault, it was because the
monkey looked shivery.

And anyway I do not
care, because I think I am
definitely the best **FRIEND**
TO THE ANIMALS EVER

and I will take the shoebox palace and the beetles in to show Miss Patterson on Meat-Free Monday and she will send me to Mr. Schumann for a gold star, and maybe I will even get to meet Griff Hunt who is on *Animal SOS* because my beetles have **MIRACULOUSLY** not died.

⭐ ⭐ ⭐ ⭐

Only when I get to school on Monday, Miss Patterson says in fact it is wrong to keep minibeasts **COOPED UP**, even inside a shoebox palace, because they are meant to be **FREE** and roaming the

WILDS and it is indeed **MIRACULOUS** that they are still alive. Only Henry Potts says they are not **ALL** alive because, look, one is on his back. So I say he is just having a **NAP** because he is very tired from the **ARDUOUS JOURNEY** to school. Only Henry Potts pokes him and he is definitely dead after all. And so Miss Patterson says at break I must go completely quickly to the Nature Garden and put the thirteen beetles who are not dead on the compost.

And so at break me and Cosmo take the shoebox palace to the Nature Garden and I say, "Farewell, *it is time for you to run* **FREE** *and roam the* **WILDS**," which is the compost heap i.e. some carrot peel and a

potato with a green bit. And the beetles
absolutely do **RUN**, except for one who has a
leg stuck in the sofa, and so I rescue him **AND**
set him free and so I am even more of a
FRIEND TO THE ANIMALS.

Which is when I have my next

BRILLIANT IDEA™,

which is to set lots more minibeasts or even big beasts **FREE** to roam the **WILDS**, and Cosmo agrees and so off we go to find some.

And we have only gone maybe four steps when we find a beast and it is Marlon, the school goat, who is inside a special fence made by Mr. Eggs (who is our caretaker and who smells of dog), otherwise he eats a lot of things he should not be eating (Marlon not Mr. Eggs) e.g.:

a) Cosmo's satsuma.

2. Alexander Pringle's jam sandwich.

iii) Alexander Pringle.

But I say it is not very **FRIENDLY** that
Marlon is **COOPED UP** inside the special fence,
and Cosmo agrees, because his mum Sunflower is
very **KEEN** on animal rights and Cosmo says this
is almost definitely an **ANIMAL WRONG** and so
we must **RELEASE** him completely quickly.

And so I unlatch the gate and am just wondering where some good **WILDS** are for Marlon to roam, e.g. our back garden, when Mr. Schumann shouts very loudly,

Penelope Jones, will you step **AWAY** from the goat enclosure, that is the fifth time this term.

And so I do step away and then I have to step straight back to our class, and for the rest of the morning I do not even think about releasing any more beasts because I am too busy racking my head to think of facts about Queen Victoria.

Only just as I am thinking about whether in fact Queen Victoria would have had roller skates, because it would be quite tricky skating in a long dress (and I know this because I have tried roller skating in Mum's nightie and now the skates are in the **OUT OF BOUNDS** cupboard and the nightie is in the recycling bin), something **ODD** happens, which is that the light in the locust tank goes off and so do all the computers and so does the vacuum cleaner which Mr. Eggs is using to clean up the polystyrene peanuts from the shoebox palace.

And almost immediately everyone is "OOH"ing and "AAH"ing and wondering who has taken away the electricity, and Henry Potts says it is most possibly Optimus Prime, leader of the Autobots, who is going to use it to **DOMINATE THE WORLD** (because he is very **KEEN** on Optimus Prime and on dominating the world). But Cosmo says it is most possibly Maximus Terror, leader of the Zombiebots, who is going to use it to dominate Optimus Prime and also Henry Potts.

But Miss Patterson says it is more probably a **GLITCH** or a **GREMLIN** and to stop **SPECULATING** and start washing our hands, because it is time for meat-free lunch and it is vegetarian sausages.

Only when we get to the hall with our clean hands, another **ODD** thing happens, which is that Mrs. Feast 1 (who is the dinner lady and who once wore slippers to school) says the vegetarian sausages have gone mysteriously **MISSING**, and so it is macaroni cheese and it is a jolly good thing she boiled the macaroni before the electricity went out or it would be just some cheese, which is against council rules (because she is very **KEEN** on council rules).

QUEUE
THIS WAY

And so then we are all guessing like **MAD** who has taken the sausages, i.e.:

a) Mrs. Feast 2 (who is the other dinner lady and who is the sister-in-law of Mrs. Feast 1) says it is probably **THIEVES** or **VANDALS**.

2. I say it is a **GLITCH** or a **GREMLIN**.

3. Cosmo says no, it is definitely **MAXIMUS TERROR**, who is using the sausages to **DOMINATE** our school and we will all be zombies by numeracy time.

Which is when Bridget Grimes starts to weep because she is not **KEEN** on **ZOMBIES** or **THIEVES** or **MACARONI CHEESE**. Only Mr. Schumann, who is not

KEEN on council rules or on Mrs. Feast 1 or 2 or on weeping, says it is not **THIEVES** or **VANDALS** or **MAXIMUS TERROR** who have stolen the sausages, they are probably just **VICTIMS** of the **SYSTEM**, i.e. they are lost somewhere in the big fridge, and to sit down on our bottoms and eat our macaroni before it goes cold.

And so we are all sitting on our bottoms eating meat-free macaroni (except for Bridget Grimes, who is poking it with a fork, and Alexander Pringle, who is eating a jam sandwich) when something else **MYSTERIOUS** happens, which is that a noise starts coming from the **CONFISCATION CUPBOARD**, which is where Mr. Schumann

CONFISCATION CUPBOARD

keeps all the things that should not have come to school in the first place, e.g.:

a) Cherry Scarpelli's mobile phone, which has seven different ringtones and one of them is "The Hokey-Cokey".

2. Jamal Malik's little brother Shoaib (only he did not go in the cupboard, he went in Mr. Schumann's office, although I think Mr. Schumann wishes it had been the cupboard because he broke the swivelly chair).

Only the noise from the cupboard does not sound one bit like a mobile phone or even Jamal Malik's brother Shoaib, because it is **MUCH** more **MYSTERIOUS** than that. And Luke Bruce, who can hang upside down by one leg from the climbing frame, says it is **JABBA THE HUTT**. But Henry Potts says it is not **JABBA THE HUTT**, it is a **WEREWOLF** who is actually Mrs. Butterworth from the post office because she has a moustache.

And Cosmo says it is not **JABBA THE HUTT** or a **WEREWOLF** that is actually Mrs. Butterworth, it is the **GHOST** of a **DEAD HEADMASTER** (because he is very **KEEN** on ghosts and also dead headmasters). Only Mr. Schumann (who is **NOT** keen on dead headmasters) says it is not **JABBA THE HUTT** or a **WEREWOLF** or a **GHOST** because they are **NOT REAL**, and in fact there is probably a very **SIMPLE** explanation and he will open the door and **REVEAL** it.

And Mr. Schumann is right, because when he opens the door he does not reveal **JABBA THE HUTT** or a **WEREWOLF** who is actually Mrs. Butterworth or a **GHOST**, he reveals Marlon, who is eating a mobile phone.

And then everyone is **FLUMMOXED** and racking their heads to think how he could have got there, when I remember about unlatching Marlon's gate and Mr. Schumann telling me to step away. Which I tell Mr. Schumann, but for once he does not have time to be **SICK AND TIRED** because almost immediately there is **MAYHEM**, because Marlon sees that Bridget Grimes has still got some macaroni cheese on her plate and he is very **KEEN** on macaroni cheese so he runs completely quickly to it, which makes Bridget scream, which makes Marlon do a goat noise and also some poo that looks like chocolate drops.

And so everyone is saying "EWW!" except Henry Potts, who says,

Do not fear, Bridget, I will capture the dreaded Marlon and be a **HERO**!

(Because he is very **KEEN** on being a **HERO**.)

Only Cosmo says, "Do not fear, Marlon, I will capture the dreaded Henry Potts and be a **HERO**." And so

Cosmo dives on Henry,

who dives on Bridget Grimes,

who dives into a plate of macaroni cheese,

which scares Marlon,
who does some more
poo and runs out of
the hall and down
the corridor and into
the playground,

which is where he
stays all afternoon
while Mr. Eggs
tries to catch
him with a net
and some
bits of
macaroni.

93

✦ ✧ ✦ ✦

So when I get home I am completely full of
GLOOM because I have lost three gold stars.
Daisy says,

It is all your own
fault, Penelope Jones,
you are such a
complete **MORON**.

And Dad calls me Penny Dreadful and does
the honking goose laugh, but I do not see
the funny side because I was only trying to
be a **FRIEND TO THE ANIMALS** and now
Marlon will be locked behind the special
fence for ever.

But for once I am wrong, because the next day Marlon has mysteriously **DISAPPEARED**, only he is not in the confiscated cupboard, he is on a farm with some sheep and a llama where he can be **FREE** and **ROAM THE WILDS** and also not eat macaroni cheese or vegetarian sausages or the fuse box.

And it was all Mr. Schumann's idea, so in fact it is he who is the best **FRIEND TO THE ANIMALS EVER**.

Penny Dreadful

Becomes a Bridesmaid

Daisy is my big sister,

and she is normally very irritating, e.g. when she is saying stuff like:

But at the moment she is doubly irritating because Lucy B. Finnegan, who is her best friend (except when they have had an argument about orange socks, for instance) is being a bridesmaid for the seventh time and Daisy has not even been a bridesmaid **ONCE**.

I say she is **MAD** because weddings are **FUSS** and **BOTHER** and I am never going to get married, not **EVEN** to Cosmo Moon Webster, not **EVEN** if he invents the first-ever time machine made out of a bus, some tinfoil and an alarm clock.

And Cosmo is not getting married either because his mum Sunflower does not believe in weddings, she believes in **FREEDOM** and **SELF EXPRESSION** and also **FAIRIES**.

But Daisy says in fact it is I who am **MAD** because weddings have **CAKE** and **KISSING**, and she is very keen on cake and especially kissing because she is going to marry George Helmet, who has the longest legs in Year Seven, and they will definitely kiss and have a cake and it will be three layers tall with white icing and real diamonds on it.

And Dad says,

Ooh, cake — did I ever tell you I could have been a baker if I hadn't married your mum. Maybe I will make a chocolate log immediately.

But Mum says no he could not have been and no he will not because he burns even biscuits and also she has had it **UP TO HERE**, what with Aunt Deedee ringing fourteen times this morning only Mum cannot hear what she's saying because someone has superglued a pincushion onto the holes (which was not completely my fault, it was because Mum said she was **UP TO HERE** with Dr. Cement calling her about gromits and she was the one with earache). Only now Mum will have to go round there to find out what the **HOO-HAH** is, so could we please stop arguing about weddings and go and do something constructive instead.

And so we do and it is called betting, which Gran has taught us all about, and which we are very **KEEN** on at the moment, e.g.:

a) I bet Daisy a jumping bean that is only a bit broken that she cannot stand on her hands for seventeen seconds and she cannot so I win.

ii) Daisy bets me a sticker shaped like a tomato which has not completely lost its stick that I cannot hold my breath for seventeen minutes and I cannot so she wins.

3. Gran bets both of us fifty pence and a chocolate digestive that we cannot be **QUIET** and **STILL** for a whole episode of *Animal SOS* and Daisy can but I cannot so Gran half wins and so does Daisy but I am empty-handed.

But today Daisy bets me something super-special and it is her sparkly tights and I can have them if I can drink a glass of chocolate milk upside down without spilling any on the carpet. And I am very **KEEN** on her special sparkly tights (because they make me look like Dr. Demonica, who is always freezing people with her evil heart of ice, only Magnificent Marvin melts her heart with his flamethrowing fingers, and so she is nice to everybody until the next episode) so I say,

Bet **ACCEPTED**.

And I drink the glass of chocolate milk, only most of it goes on the carpet and also on my shoes and so I do not get sparkly tights

but I do get tutted at by Dad, who says I will be in **BIG TROUBLE** when Mum gets home and it is lucky he is so good at **CLEANING** things and in fact he could have been a professional cleaner if he hadn't married Mum because he always gets things **SPARKLY** bright.

And so everything is all **SPARKLY**, except for my legs because of the no tights, which means I am completely cross. And that is why I have my first **BRILLIANT IDEA™**, which is to bet Daisy something she cannot possibly win and then I will get the tights for sure and so I say,

> I bet that you will not be a bridesmaid in the next three days and if I win I get the tights and if you win you get a year's supply of sponge fingers.

Because I am not **KEEN** on sponge fingers but
Mum is always buying them. But Daisy says
I am **MAD** if I think that she will **ACCEPT**
that bet and she bets me the tights that I will
not be a bridesmaid in the next three weeks.
And so I say I bet her a horse called Horace
that she will not be a bridesmaid in the next
three years. And then she is just trying to
work out what comes after three years when a
COINCIDENCE happens (which is not the
same as a **CONSPIRACY** because I have
checked with Mr. Schumann), which is that at
that very moment Mum comes back from
Aunt Deedee's and it turns out the **HOO-HAH**
is that she is getting married to Mr. Bentley-
Bucket (who is not a vampire after all, which

is completely another story), and we are
BOTH going to be bridesmaids and so is
Georgia May Morton-Jones, who is my
cousin and who shows potential on the violin,
and so is someone called James Pants, only
he is not a bridesmaid, he is a **PAGEBOY**.
And so Daisy is as **PLEASED AS PUNCH**.

But she says Aunt Deedee is **MAD**
for letting me be a bridesmaid.

And I say Aunt Deedee
is **MAD** for
letting Daisy be
a bridesmaid.

And Mum says the only
person who is **MAD** is Mr.
Bentley-Bucket for marrying
Aunt Deedee, who is mostly sacking
people for **NOT MEASURING UP**, so it will
probably be all over before the wedding.

And I say when is
the wedding and it
is in three weeks so
in fact we both win.

Only I do not get the tights,
and Daisy does not get the sponge
fingers and no one gets a horse
called Horace because we are both
in **BIG TROUBLE**, because it turns
out Dad could not have been a
professional cleaner after all
because he forgot to make my
shoes sparkly bright and there are
chocolate footprints in the front
room and in the back room and
also on the bathroom wall (which
is not completely my fault, it is
because Daisy bet me I couldn't
walk up it like a fly and I cannot).

✫ ✫ ✫ ✫

And so I am completely **GLOOMY** because from then on it is **WEDDINGS**, **WEDDINGS**, **WEDDINGS**, which means on Saturday it is **NOT** going to Cosmo's house to see if there is a secret tunnel under the floorboards, it is going to see Mrs. Gutteridge to fetch my bridesmaid's dress which is made of white itchy stuff and no I may **NOT** wear it to school and pretend I am a ghost.

And the Saturday after that it is **NOT** going to poke the dead pigeon behind the post office, it is going to Hedges & Blunt in Chipping Broadley to get a wedding present, which is ten spoons (which is **MAD** if you ask me because who needs ten spoons at once, and wouldn't a tortoise be better for instance, but Mum says no it would not).

And the Saturday after that it is the **WEDDING**, which means **NO** doing lots of interesting stuff because I have to hold hands with James Pants and he will not want to be doing that if I have mud, or marshmallows, or a bit of a frog on them.

Only I say I am not **KEEN** on holding hands with James Pants because what if he smells of dog, for instance, (like Mr. Eggs, who is our caretaker) and in fact I would rather **PERISH**. Only Mum says he will not smell of dog if Aunt Deedee has anything to do with it, he will smell of soap and lots of it.

. And I say how much does she **BET** he will smell of soap and she says she is not a betting woman, but Dad says he is a betting woman

(only not a woman) and he bets me a trip to
Monkey Madness that the wedding will be **FUN**,
I will see. And Mum says she bets he will regret
saying that, only I say she is not a betting
woman so she is not allowed to say anything,
which is when she looks like she is about to say
something that **SHE** might regret. Only luckily
Gran says,

Lawks, is that
the time?

And it is, and it is thirteen minutes past eleven and we were supposed to be at the church at eleven o'clock and so Aunt Deedee will be going **MAD** and so will Mr. Bentley-Bucket and so will Reverend Bruton the vicar, who has to christen Brady O'Grady's little brother Anfield at one o'clock so there had better not be any **DILLY-DALLYING**.

And so we absolutely do not **DILLY-DALLY** but we get a bag of rice for throwing because it is good luck, only our rice is mostly gone from the time I tried to see if it was true that pigeons exploded if they ate it and it is not, and so we have to get some very small pasta shaped like worms, but Mum says Aunt Deedee will be too **FILLED WITH HAPPINESS** to notice.

And then we go completely quickly to the church and there is Georgia May Morton-Jones with a basket full of pink petals and there is James Pants with a black shiny suit on and brown shiny hair and there is Aunt Deedee with a face like **THUNDER**. But luckily there is no time to be **CROSS**, which is not a **COINCIDENCE** but is **CONVENIENT**, because Aunt Deedee says,

And we are quick-marching all the way up the aisle when James Pants says something very interesting, which is,

I bet you trip someone up.

And I say,

I bet **YOU** trip someone up.

And James Pants says,
"Bet **ACCEPTED**."
And so do I.
And so I am
concentrating
very hard
on **NOT**
tripping but

what happens is that I forget which is left-right and which is right-left and I get it wrong and I do trip someone over and it is me, and James says, "I win."
And I say, "Don't."
And James Pants says, "Do." And Aunt Deedee says,

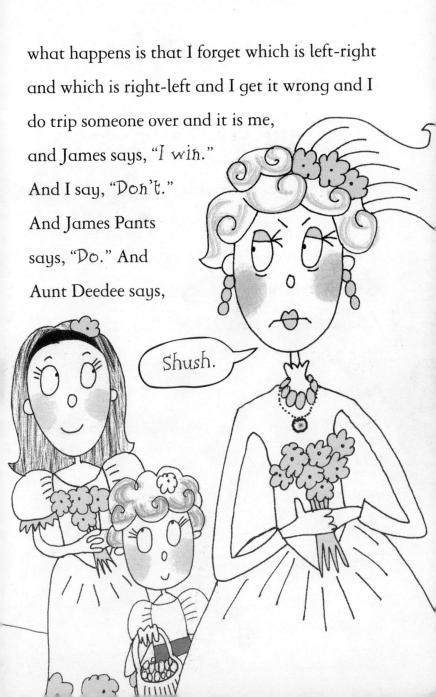

Shush.

But I do not mind the shushing because
I have had a

BRILLIANT IDEA™,

which is to do betting with James Pants because
it is more interesting than the vicar, i.e.
Reverend Bruton, who is banging on about
something to do with the bones of a man called
Adam. And so I am **RACKING MY HEAD** to
think of a good bet and I think of three and
they are:

a) Who can invent a cloak of invisibility so
that we can hide in it and go outside and
dangle upside down from the conker tree?

b) Who can throw a piece of very-small-
pasta-shaped-like-a-worm the furthest (because

Aunt Deedee said no throwing of rice but she did **NOT** say no throwing of very-small-pasta-shaped-like-a-worm)?

3. Who can make Aunt Deedee scream?

And so I tell them all to James Pants and he says **BETS ACCEPTED**, only not number **a)** because we will also need a rabbit and a magic hat, and not number **3.** because what if Aunt Deedee screams so loud that Mr. Bentley-Bucket goes deaf and he cannot hear Reverend Bruton say "You are now husband and lady, etc." and so the wedding is **NULL AND VOID**, which means not happening. And so it is only one bet accepted really, and it is the throwing-a-very-small-piece-of-pasta-shaped-like-a-worm.

And so we are throwing the very-small-pieces-of-pasta-shaped-like-a-worm and I hit:

a) A tapestry of the Angel Gabriel

2. Some pink flowers on a table

3. Daisy's shoe

And James Pants hits:

1. A display of things made of raffia

2. A wooden eagle

c) Mrs. Dullforce, who plays the organ

Which is definitely the furthest, so he wins bet number **b)**. But that is not all, because it also makes Mrs. Dullforce hit a note on the organ which makes Aunt Deedee scream, luckily not loud enough for Mr. Bentley-Bucket to go deaf, but loud enough for the best man, who is called Rolf, to let go of the wedding ring in fright, which pings through

the air and rolls onto the floor somewhere near
Mrs. Butterworth from the post office. And so
James is as **PLEASED AS PUNCH** because he is
SUPREME CHAMPION of betting. But someone
is not and that is Aunt Deedee because she says
she needs the ring to get
married or it will be
NULL AND VOID.

And it is lucky Mrs. Butterworth has a beady eye because she finds it under Phoebe Patterson-Parry. And then the wedding is back on and there is kissing and everyone shouts hurrah and throws rice, except me and James who shout "Yuck" and do not throw anything, not even small pieces of pasta shaped like worms, because Mrs. Butterworth's beady eye has also seen who threw the pasta and so it is confiscated.

But I do not mind because I have had my next **BRILLIANT IDEA™**, which is for bet number 4, which is who can find the best thing that is **BORROWED** and that is also **BLUE**, because it is very important to have four things at your wedding and they have to be one old, one new, one borrowed and one blue. And so Aunt Deedee is wearing Gran's sapphire necklace, which is old and borrowed and blue all at once, which is **CLEVER**, which is why she is a **BUSINESS MOGUL** and Dad does traffic cones.

And James Pants says **BET ACCEPTED** and we will do it at the reception which is at Aunt Deedee's house, which will make it especially tricky because of all the rules, e.g.:

1. No eating except at the table.

ii) No plasticine or paint or glue except at the table and only if is covered in a plastic cloth.

c) No eating plasticine or paint or glue.

Plus if you even **LOOK** at a glass candlestick she says, "Do not even think about it, Penelope Jones".

And so when we get to Aunt Deedee's house I am definitely **NOT** looking at the glass candlesticks, not **EVEN** the blue ones, but what I **AM** looking at is a white cake that is three layers tall and on each layer is icing and not real diamonds but silver balls, and on the top it

also has a plastic man and a plastic woman
and a sign saying **CONGRATULATIONS** and
it is blue. Which is when I have my next
BRILLIANT IDEA™, which is that the sign
will be my thing that is borrowed and also blue
and it will be better than James Pants's thing,
and so I will be **SUPREME
CHAMPION** of betting after all.

So I am **SCOOTING** towards the cake
when Aunt Deedee appears in front
of me and says,

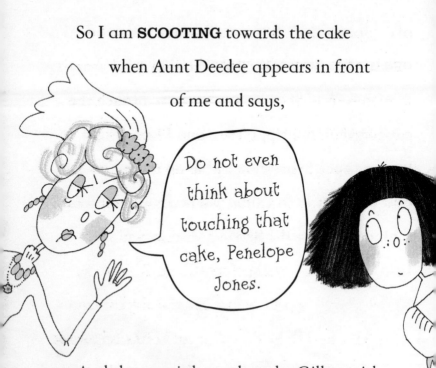

Do not even think about touching that cake, Penelope Jones.

And she says it has taken the Gilbey girls
seven hours to get the icing smooth and with no
bumps and in fact she will **MOVE** the cake out
of the way until the cake-cutting ceremony
because it will mean temptation is out of the
way too. And so she does and the cake is on top

of a cupboard in the kitchen where it can be **SEEN AND NOT TOUCHED** by any small hands. Which is true, because I cannot even touch the cupboard on my tippy toes, and I know this because once I threw a marble up there and I could not get it down for two hours until it rolled a bit and fell on the head of Valeria Smirnov (who was the au pair before Katya Romanov, who was the au pair before Lilya Bobylev) and so Valeria had to lie down for an hour and forgot to make tea and so Aunt Deedee sacked her.

But Mr. Schumann, who is mostly saying that he is **SICK** and **TIRED** and it is mostly of me, is also saying something else and it is that we can do **ANYTHING** if we **PUT OUR MINDS TO IT**. And so I completely put my mind to it

and amazingly it works because my mind
thinks of an answer and it is: o O O

> If you pull that little table next to the
> cupboard, and then put a chair on the
> table, and another chair on the chair on
> the table, then you will be able to reach
> the sign which is the best thing borrowed
> and blue, and you won't even have to
> touch the icing on the cake, not one bit.

And so I do. I move the table next to the
cupboard and on top of that I put a chair and
then I realize if I just stretch a bit I won't need the
other chair, which is lucky because Mrs. Nugent is
sitting on it, and then I climb up the **AMAZING
TOWER** and I am teetering a bit this way and a

bit that way but I am **NOT** falling off **OR** touching the icing at all. And I am **JUST** stretching up to get the sign which is borrowed and blue when a **COINCIDENCE** happens, which is that Aunt Deedee comes into the kitchen and sees me and says in a very shouty voice,

What are you **DOING**, Penelope Jones?

So if you think about it, it is all her fault for being so loud. Because what happens is, I am so **SURPRISED** at the shouty voice that I do a little wobble, which makes the

AMAZING TOWER do a little wobble, which makes me do a bigger wobble right into the cake in three layers, which does an even **BIGGER** wobble, and in fact it is so big it wobbles off the cupboard and onto the head of Dad who has come in to get some orange juice.

And then quite a lot of other things happen and it mostly involves more shouty voices and they are mostly at me. And Dad calls me Penny Dreadful and does the honking goose laugh, which makes cake fly out of his mouth

and hit Aunt Deedee on the nose, who does an
even shoutier voice and tells us it is high time
we all went home.

＊ ＊ ＊ ＊

When we get home Mum is completely cross
and says it is definitely the last wedding she's
going to because they are too much **FUSS** and
BOTHER and amazingly Daisy agrees.

But I do **NOT**, because in my hand is the blue
sign after all, which means I win the bet because
James Pants only got a sock that is Dr. Cement's,
and so I am the **SUPREME CHAMPION** of
betting and the wedding is **FUN** after all. And
THAT means I also win a trip to Monkey
Madness, which Dad completely regrets because
this time the monkeys steal his watch (which was
not completely my fault, I was just seeing if they
could tell the time) and so Mum wins her bet too,
even though she is not a betting woman.

And I say I think I might get married after all and it will be to James Pants and I bet Mum a blue **CONGRATULATIONS** sign and a badge that says *I'm as mad as a monkey* that it will be **FUN**.

The End

Joanna Nadin

wrote this book –
and lots of others
like it. She is small,
funny, clever,
sneaky and musical.
Before she became a writer, she wanted to be a
champion ballroom dancer or a jockey, but she
was actually a lifeguard at a swimming pool,
a radio newsreader, a cleaner in an old people's
home, and a juggler. She likes Marmite on toast
for mains breakfast, and jam on toast for
pudding. Her perfect day would involve baking,
surfing, sitting in cafes in Paris, and playing
with her daughter – who reminds her a lot of
Penny Dreadful…

Jess Mikhail

illustrated this book.
She loves creating funny
characters with bright
colours and fancy

patterns to make people smile.
Her favourite place is her tiny home, where she
lives with her tiny dog and spends lots of time
drawing, scanning, scribbling, printing, stamping,
and sometimes using her scary computer. She
loves to rummage through a good car boot sale
or a charity shop to find weird and
wonderful things. A perfect day for
her would have to involve a sunny
beach and large amounts of curry
and ice cream (not together).

For Menace 2,
who is an excellent causer of hoo-hah,
but an utter inspiration.

First published in the UK in 2013 by Usborne Publishing Ltd., Usborne House,
83-85 Saffron Hill, London EC1N 8RT, England. www.usborne.com

Copyright © Joanna Nadin, 2013
Illustrations copyright © Usborne Publishing Ltd., 2013

The right of Joanna Nadin to be identified as the author of this work has been asserted by her in
accordance with the Copyright, Designs and Patents Act, 1988.

The name Usborne and the devices 🎈🪂 are Trade Marks of Usborne Publishing Ltd.

A CIP catalogue record for this book is available from the British Library.

JFMAMJJ SOND/13

ISBN 9781409554554 02845/1
Printed in Reading, Berkshire, UK.